Contents

KV-703-524

Introduction

'Mr President, there appears to be a bit of a problem ... More than thirty of our bombers have been ordered to attack their targets inside Russia. The planes are all carrying nuclear bombs.'

Crazy General Ripper, of the US Air Force, has sent his planes to destroy the USSR, and nobody knows how to stop them. The US President's advisers meet to discuss how they can save the world from nuclear war. Then the Russian Ambassador tells them about the Doomsday Machine, and they realize that the situation is even worse than they thought. While the President speaks to the Russian leader, who is drunk, on the telephone, the mysterious Dr Strangelove makes plans for the future.

Stanley Kubrick's *Dr Strangelove* (1964) is one of the most famous films ever made. It is a frightening warning that nuclear war might start by mistake, and that governments might not be able to control their own forces. But it is also a very funny story, with some unforgettable characters, including the war-loving Major 'King' Kong, the mad General Ripper, the very English Group Captain Lionel Mandrake and, of course, Dr Strangelove himself.

The idea for the film came from Peter George's more serious book, *Red Alert*. After working with Kubrick on the film, Peter George wrote the book again as *Dr Strangelove*. He died in 1965.

Dr Strangelove

Or:

How I learned to stop worrying and love the bomb

Adapted from the novel by
PETER GEORGE
Based on the screenplay by
STANLEY KUBRICK,
PETER GEORGE and
TERRY SOUTHERN

Level 4

Retold by David Bowker
Series Editors: Andy Hopkins and Jocelyn Potter

Pearson Education Limited
Edinburgh Gate, Harlow,
Essex CM20 2JE, England
and Associated Companies throughout the world.

ISBN 0 582 43940 X

First published in Great Britain by Souvenir Press Ltd.,
by arrangement with Barnes & Noble, Inc., USA
This edition first published 2001

Typeset by Ferdinand Pageworks, London
Set in 11/14pt Bembo
Printed in Spain by Mateu Cromo, S. A. Pinto (Madrid)

Published by Pearson Education Limited in association with
Penguin Books Ltd, both companies being subsidiaries of Pearson Plc

For a complete list of the titles available in the Penguin Readers series please write to your local
Pearson Education office or to: Marketing Department, Penguin Longman Publishing,
5 Bentinck Street, London W1M 5RN.

Chapter 1   Condition Red

Leper Colony

At the time of our story, the US and the USSR were afraid of each other. They especially feared a surprise nuclear attack. To protect itself, the US kept seventy jet bombers in the air at all times. Each aeroplane carried two nuclear bombs and had a separate target in the USSR, which it would only fly to if there was an attack. If there was no attack, the bombers turned round at their Fail-Safe point,* when they were still about two thousand kilometres from their targets, and flew home.

On this day, a new group of thirty-five bombers had left Burpelson Air Force Base many hours before. One of them was named *Leper Colony*, and the six men inside were looking forward to turning round and going home. In the pilot's seat sat Major 'King' Kong, reading a magazine, and on his right Captain 'Ace' Owens was looking out at the sky and eating an apple. He was bored. Behind them Lieutenant Dietrich, the defence officer, was playing with a pack of cards, while Lieutenant Goldberg, the radar/radio officer, was reading a book. Below them sat the navigator, Lieutenant Kivel, and the man who had to drop the bombs, Lieutenant Zogg.

Lieutenant Kivel looked at his maps and switched on his intercom.

'Three minutes to the turning point, King. New direction will be three-five-three.'

Three minutes later, King turned the plane. The men were

---

* Fail-Safe point: the planes must not go further than this point. This is to make sure that they do not start a war by accident.

pleased to be going home after fourteen hours in the air. Suddenly, Goldberg sat up. On his radio he was receiving a coded message from Burpelson. While he looked through his code book, he said, 'I've got a message from base, King.'

King was thinking about a beautiful woman he was planning to spend the night with. He said, 'What do *they* want?'

'We have to stay here at the Fail-Safe point,' said Goldberg.

All the men were annoyed. King turned to Ace Owens.

'Boy,' he said, 'if we stay here too long, we'll miss our date. You know that, don't you?'

'Yes,' said Ace Owens sadly.

King angrily turned the plane again, sixteen kilometres above the icy sea north of Russia.

Burpelson Air Force Base

It was a quiet, peaceful night at Burpelson Air Force Base. The stars shone brightly through the clear desert air. Twenty metres below ground, Group Captain Lionel Mandrake sat in the Operations Centre. Mandrake was in the British Royal Air Force and he had been at Burpelson for more than a year. He enjoyed it, though it was not always easy to understand the strange sense of humour of his commanding officer, General Ripper. Mandrake was watching the hands of the big wall clock slowly move round when the phone rang. It was General Ripper.

'Now listen to me very carefully, Group Captain. I'm putting the base on Condition Red.'

Mandrake was surprised. 'Condition Red, sir? What's happened?'

For a few seconds there was silence. Mandrake wondered if perhaps the General had put the phone down, but then Ripper spoke again. He said slowly, 'It looks like we're in a world war.'

'A world war, sir?'

'Yes, Group Captain. I'm afraid this looks like it's going to be *it*.'

'Good Lord!' Mandrake said. 'Have they hit anything yet?'

'Group Captain, that's all I've been told. Now, you know the plan?'

'The plan, sir?'

'That's right, Group Captain. Operation Oyster.'

'Oh, that! Yes, sir,' Mandrake said enthusiastically. He thought quickly about Operation Oyster and what he had to do.

'And get the Go-code out to the boys,' Ripper said.

Mandrake said, 'The Go-code, sir?'

'Yeah, yeah, yeah. Go-code, Ultech. The code for the message to attack.'

'Yes, sir. You will have to give me the code, General.'

Ripper said, 'What's the matter, Group Captain, don't you have it?'

'No, sir. I believe you're the only one on the base who knows it.'

General Ripper looked at the papers on his desk.

'You're quite right, Group Captain,' he said. 'It is Fox-George-Dog, Fox-George-Dog. Please repeat.'

Mandrake repeated the code.

'Good,' Ripper said, 'very good. When you've done that, I want you to come up here to my office.'

'But,' said Mandrake, 'if I do that, there'll be no one in control down here.'

'*Are you questioning my orders, Group Captain?*' said Ripper angrily.

'No, sir. Of course not,' Mandrake replied quickly.

Ripper breathed deeply three times. Then he said, 'You're a good officer, Group Captain, but I am in command here and when I give orders I expect them to be obeyed. Perhaps we do things a bit differently than you do in the RAF.'

That, Mandrake thought, was very true. But General Ripper

3

was his commanding officer and he replied loyally, 'Yes, sir, of course.'

'All right then. I want you to get reports on base security. Send soldiers to defend the roads coming into the base. These Commies* are very clever, and they may attack us.'

Mandrake said loudly, 'Yes, sir.'

Ripper put down his phone. Maybe soon he could relax, maybe even have a small drink of alcohol and pure water. But that was for later. There was still lots of work to do. He picked up another of his telephones.

Chapter 2   Code Ultech

Leper Colony

Inside *Leper Colony*, which was now circling gently around its Fail-Safe point, Lieutenant Goldberg received another coded message on the radio. He studied his code book for a few moments and then switched on his intercom.

'Hey, King,' he said. 'I've just had a message from base. It says, "Attack using Ultech."'

King repeated the message to himself. '*Now* what are they talking about?'

'Attack using Ultech,' Goldberg repeated. 'That's exactly what it says.'

Captain Ace Owens put down his magazine. He looked across at King.

---

* Commies: this word, short for 'communists', was used especially by people who did not like the communist governments of Russia, China and other countries. Communists believe that all people are equal and that the workers should control the economy.

'Is he joking?'

King said, 'Well, check your code again – that just can't be right.'

'I *have* checked it again,' Goldberg said.

King stood up slowly, then said, 'Goldberg, you've made a mistake.'

'If you don't believe me,' Goldberg said angrily, 'come and see.'

The other men had heard this conversation, and they all left their places to join King as he stood next to Goldberg.

Goldberg held out the code book to King.

'Here,' he said, 'you want to check it yourself?'

King looked at the book quickly, then he said, 'All right, just ask them to repeat it.'

The men watched as the message came back exactly as before. There were a few moments of complete silence while they thought about it. Their faces became very serious. Slowly they all turned towards King.

King spoke quietly. 'Well, boys, I think this is it.'

'What?' said Ace Owens.

'War.'

'But we're carrying nuclear bombs,' Zogg whispered.

'That's right,' said King. '*Nuclear* war.'

Zogg said, with hope in his voice, 'Maybe it's just an exercise, to see if we're ready. It could be a sort of loyalty test. You know, give the Go-code and then the Recall, just to find out who would actually go.'

'Now listen to me, Zogg,' King said, 'that's the Go-code! It's never been given to anyone before and it would never be given as a test.'

King went back to the pilot's seat. The others continued to discuss the matter quietly.

'It's going to be difficult for the people back home,' Kivel said.

'Yeah,' Dietrich agreed, 'really difficult.'

5

Ace Owens said, 'But how did it start? I can't understand it.'

Goldberg was becoming excited. 'I believe they hit us!' he said.

'That's right!' Dietrich said loudly.

King turned round and looked at them from his seat. He said calmly but coldly, 'OK, so we've been hit. All right, so what do we do now? I'll tell you what we do. We've got to hit them back! Isn't that right?'

Dietrich and Goldberg looked at each other. King was right, they both realized that.

Dietrich opened a box and pulled out a thick envelope marked 'Ultech'. He held it up so King could see it. King looked at it carefully.

'OK,' he said, 'open it.' He watched as Dietrich opened the envelope and took out six smaller envelopes, one for each man.

Kivel, the navigator, said through the intercom, 'First direction is one-seven-five.'

King made a change to the instruments in front of him, and the bomber began to turn. Then King read from his orders.

'OK. No more radio contact except to receive the coded recall message from base. Our first target is the nuclear missile base at Laputa. If there are problems with the first bomb, we'll use the second one. If not, we'll go to our second target, the missile base at Borchav. Any questions?'

The men had no questions.

King continued. 'OK. Now, in about ten minutes we'll start going down to keep under their radar. We'll cross over the coast at about five thousand metres, then drop lower to the first target. OK, boys, now how about some hot coffee?'

Washington

The Fabulous Hotel was large, ugly and expensive. Most of the guests were top government officers, military chiefs and politicians. On the seventeenth floor, in room 1704, General Buck Turgidson, the most important of the military chiefs, was enjoying a cool and relaxing shower while his secretary was lying on her stomach on the bed. She was tall and good-looking and she was wearing very little.

Over the sound of General Turgidson singing under the shower, a telephone rang. The secretary switched off the sun lamp over the bed and picked up the phone.

'Hello ... Oh, yes, General Turgidson is here, but I'm afraid he can't come to the phone right now ... Oh, this is his secretary, Miss Wood. Freddie, how are you? ... Just fine, thank you ... Oh, we were just doing some of the General's paperwork ... Well, listen, Freddie, he can't come to the phone ... Oh, I see, just a second.'

She shouted across the room, 'General Turgidson, Colonel Puntrich is on the phone. He says it can't wait.'

Turgidson shouted from the bathroom, 'Find out what he wants.'

The girl said quickly into the telephone, 'Freddie, the General's in the bathroom right now. Could you tell me what it's about?'

She listened for a few moments and then shouted towards the bathroom, 'Buck, they heard a coded message about eight minutes ago from Burpelson Air Force Base. It was being sent to the bombers. It said: Ultech – Attack.'

The shower was turned off. Turgidson was annoyed. He said, 'Er ... um ... tell him to call what's-his-name ... the base commander, Ripper. Do I have to think of everything?'

Miss Wood said, 'Freddie, are you there? Well listen, the General suggests you call General Ripper ... Oh I see ... You mean all communications are dead?'

General Turgidson came out of the bathroom. He took the telephone from his secretary, who reached for a cigarette from her handbag.

Turgidson said, 'Fred, Buck here. What's happening? Ah . . . ah yeah . . . Is it really Ultech? . . . Well, have we been threatened? . . . No!'

He moved his head to the right to allow his secretary to put a cigarette in his mouth. 'We haven't been threatened? . . . I don't like this, Fred . . . Ah, yeah . . . Well, I'll tell you what you'd better do. Phone Elmo and Charlie, put everything on Condition Red and wait by the phone. I'll call you back.' He put the phone down.

Miss Wood looked at him. Her big, liquid eyes were full of love. She said, 'What's happened?'

Turgidson said, 'Nothing. Where are my clothes?'

'On the floor. Where are you going?'

Turgidson picked up his underwear from the floor. 'Nowhere special. I just thought I'd go over to the War Room and see what's happening there.'

'But it's three o'clock in the morning!'

Turgidson quickly put on his clothes. He said, 'Well, the Air Force never sleeps.'

Miss Wood reached out a hand to touch his short hair. Then she put her other arm around his neck and held him tightly.

Burpelson Air Force Base

The calm of earlier that night had been violently interrupted at Burpelson by General Ripper's orders to close and defend the base. Groups of men with guns were moving in all directions. General Ripper watched their activities from his office with satisfaction. He now had more than a thousand men guarding the base.

He turned away from the window and walked over to his desk, picked up a hand microphone and began to speak. His voice could be heard all over the base. Men paused in their activities to listen to him, because Ripper was admired by most of the men he commanded.

'... why I am speaking to you at this moment. Many of you have never seen a nuclear bomb explosion, and because of this you may be unnecessarily worried. Let me tell you, as your commanding officer, that there is little difference between an ordinary bullet and a nuclear bomb, except for their size. But there is one thing I have learned – if you are going to die, there is nothing you can do. If you die by a bullet or a bomb, it's the same thing.'

Ripper then explained the orders that had to be obeyed in Operation Oyster. These included: (a) to defend the laws of the United States whatever happened; (b) to obey without question the orders of the commanding officer; (c) to shoot anyone who tried to get into the base, even if they appeared to be friendly; (d) to believe in God and keep our bodies pure.

Ripper paused, coughed and reached for a glass of pure rainwater.

'Finally, men, as your commanding officer for the last two years, I'd like to say this. In that time, I have always expected the best from you and you have never given me anything less than that. Good luck to you all.'

He sat back in his chair and lit a cigar. He felt tired now, but he also felt very satisfied. It was done. The base was closed and defended. Operation Oyster had been started. He knew his boys would never fail him.

The door of his office opened and Group Captain Mandrake entered.

Chapter 3   The Big Board

The Pentagon

Inside the Pentagon, the home of the US Defence Department, the lights were on although it was the middle of the night. Inside the building, there were many lifts. One of these had been seen by few people. It was now going down to a level hundreds of metres below the ground floor. The doors of the lift opened and a group of ten men came out. In the middle of the group was a small electric car in which sat Merkin Muffley, President of the United States.

As the car moved along past guards with guns, President Muffley was using an electric shaver. The group stopped in front of a heavy metal door, which was guarded by three soldiers. The President, after feeling his face with his hand, put the shaver down and got out of the car.

'Good morning, Captain,' he said to one of the soldiers.

'Good morning, sir,' said the captain. 'Your security card, please.'

President Muffley put his hands in his pockets. Then he said, 'Well, I'm sorry, Captain. I'm afraid I left my wallet in my bedroom.'

He walked forward, but the captain stopped him and said, 'I'm sorry, sir, I cannot allow you to enter. Security Rules, one thirty-four-B, seven-D . . .'

'We all know that,' said the chief of the President's security men. 'This is the *President*, Captain.'

The Captain did not move. The President said, 'You do recognize me, don't you, Captain?'

'Yes, sir. I believe I do, sir, but Security Rules, one thirty-four-B, seven-D say that nobody can enter the War Room without showing their security card.'

President Muffley was embarrassed. He said, 'Captain, this is a very difficult and unfortunate situation. This is a very urgent meeting. Even minutes may be important. I can tell you personally that you may forget the rules on this occasion.'

'I'm sorry, sir. Security Rules, one thirty-four-B, seven-D . . .'

As he spoke, the security men rushed forward and fought with the three soldiers. The chief of the group stepped forward and opened the door for the President, then followed him into a large room.

The room was empty except for one chair in the centre. The President walked quickly to the chair and sat in it comfortably. Then he took out a handkerchief and blew his nose. He had a bad cold and a headache. When the President had finished using his handkerchief, the chief pressed a large switch in the wall, and the chair moved up quickly and smoothly towards the ceiling. Unfortunately, because of a mechanical problem, it stopped a few metres below the ceiling.

The President blew his nose again impatiently, looking angrily at the chief, who pressed the switch several more times. Finally, the chair moved up again and disappeared through a door in the ceiling.

The War Room

The War Room was very large and dark. On the walls were maps of the national defence situation. On the left was a map showing the north of the United States and Russia. It could show the movement of planes and missiles coming from Russia. Next was a list of US bombers that were ready to fly, with the number of US missiles and the time it would take to prepare them. On the right was a map of Russia and the area around it. This would show the movement of American bombers towards their targets. These targets, which were also shown, were mostly missile and bomber bases. Some were near big centres of population, some were not. But it was impossible to know this from the map, as centres of population were not shown.

These maps, and some others, were known as the 'Big Board'.

In the middle of the room was a very large, round table covered with green cloth. Around this table sat about thirty men, waiting for the President to appear through the door in the floor. As his chair moved up into the one empty place at the table, nearly all the men stood up. One man did not, because he was sitting in a wheelchair. His name was Dr Strangelove.

President Muffley blew his nose noisily, then said, 'Good morning, gentlemen. Please sit down.'

He looked towards General Buck Turgidson. 'So, Buck, what's happening here?'

General Turgidson stood up. He was now dressed in his full uniform, and the four stars on his shoulders shone under the lights.

He said, 'Well, Mr President, there appears to be a bit of a problem.'

The President said, 'I know that, but what is it exactly?'

Turgidson said, 'Mr President, it appears that more than thirty of our bombers have been ordered to attack their targets inside Russia. The planes are all carrying nuclear bombs. The map of Russia will show their positions. The planes will be inside Russian radar in less than twenty-five minutes from now.'

Dr Strangelove looked carefully at the President as he listened to General Turgidson's information. The President seemed worried, Strangelove thought, while Turgidson seemed confident and happy. Strangelove himself was not unhappy. Although not many people in this room knew him, he had advised the US government on defence matters for many years. In the Second World War he had worked for the German army, but he had been injured by a British bomb. He was not sure whether he disliked the British more than the Russians.

Turgidson continued. 'Yes, sir, it seems that General Ripper of

Burpelson Air Force Base – one of our best bases, sir – decided to attack the Russians with his planes.'

President Muffley said, 'This is very difficult to understand, General. I am the only person who can order the use of nuclear bombs.'

Turgidson smiled, as he always did when he was in a difficult situation.

'That's right, sir,' he said. 'But have you forgotten about Ultech, sir?'

President Muffley shook his head. 'Ultech?'

Turgidson said quickly, 'That's right, sir. Ultech. You must remember – Ultech is an emergency war plan which allows a lower level commander to order nuclear retaliation after an attack. You agreed to it, sir. We wanted to show the Russians that they could not escape retaliation if they destroyed Washington – and you, sir.'

'All right,' President Muffley said. 'Has there been any sign that the Russians are planning to attack?'

'No, sir, there has not. It seems that General Ripper made a mistake.'

The President looked at the Big Board, where the bombers could be seen moving towards Russia.

He thought for a moment, then said, 'Well, all right. But won't the planes return automatically when they reach their Fail-Safe point?'

Turgidson was still standing. He said, 'No, sir, I'm afraid not. The planes were at their Fail-Safe positions when the Go-code was given. After they fly beyond Fail-Safe, they do not need a second order to continue. They will go on until they reach their targets.'

'Well, why haven't you radioed the planes to cancel the Go-code?'

'I'm afraid we're unable to communicate with any of the aeroplanes.'

'But this is crazy,' the President said.

Turgidson smiled his smile. 'As you may remember, Mr President, when the Go-code is received, the planes' radios can only receive special coded messages. The radios will not receive any message unless it starts with the correct code.'

President Muffley said, 'Well, of course, you must know this code?'

'No, sir, I'm afraid not. Since this is an emergency war plan, the lower-level commander decides the code. The code is therefore known only to General Ripper, since he changed it just before the planes took off and gave it to the men personally.'

President Muffley said slowly, 'Then do you mean you'll be unable to recall the planes?'

'I'm afraid so, sir.'

'How soon did you say the planes would be inside Russian radar?'

'About eighteen minutes from now, sir.'

'Are you in contact with General Ripper?' The President's voice was clear and strong now.

'No, sir. General Ripper has closed his base and cut off all communications. We are unable to speak to him.'

'Then where,' the President asked, 'did you get all this information?'

'Sir, General Ripper called us soon after he gave out the Go-code. I have some of the conversation written down here. He said, "No one can bring the planes back. I suggest you send all our other bombers after them. If not, we will be totally destroyed by Commie retaliation. So let's do it – there's no other choice. God willing, we shall win and live in peace, without fear and in true health through the purity of our bodies."'

'The purity of our bodies?' said the President. 'The man's mad. Well, we're wasting time. I want to speak personally to General Ripper on the telephone.'

'I'm afraid that will be impossible, sir.'

President Muffley was getting very angry. He said, 'General, I'm beginning to have less and less interest in what you think is possible or impossible. I am in command here. General Faceman, are there any army bases near Burpelson?'

'Yes, sir,' said Faceman, a grey-haired man in his middle forties. 'I believe there's one about ten kilometres away at Alvarado.'

'Very well,' the President said. 'Phone the commanding officer yourself and tell him to move himself and his men to Burpelson within fifteen minutes from now. I want them to enter the air force base, find General Ripper, and immediately put him into telephone contact with me.'

Dr Strangelove looked at the maps. He saw that the bombers were getting closer to Russia. He was quite pleased.

Chapter 4   Joe for King

Leper Colony

Leper Colony was still flying high above the clouds and the frozen land. But now the plane had to go lower to escape Russian radar. Lieutenant Kivel looked at the clock, waited for a few seconds and then said, 'Go down at five hundred metres a minute.'

King made some changes to the instruments in front of him, and *Leper Colony* began to fly lower and lower.

'OK, ready for checks,' said King.

As his men reported that all the equipment was working well, King smiled. Nothing could stop them now.

Lieutenant Kivel said, 'In thirty seconds there will be eighty-three minutes to the first target.'

'OK,' said King. He changed his clock to eighty-three minutes.

Group Captain Mandrake walked across General Ripper's office and stopped in front of Ripper's desk.

'Sir,' he said slowly. 'I have to ask you why you have sent the planes to attack Russia.'

'Because I thought it was right, Group Captain,' Ripper said quietly.

Mandrake began to move forward, then paused as he saw that on the other side of the desk Ripper was pointing a gun at him. Mandrake stepped back.

Ripper said pleasantly, 'Now please, don't try to leave the room, Group Captain.'

Mandrake looked at the gun nervously. Ripper put it down on the desk. 'Now,' he said, 'just calm down, Group Captain Mandrake, and pour me a glass of alcohol and rain water. Have a drink yourself.'

Mandrake crossed the room and began to pour out the drinks.

Ripper watched him and said, 'Relax, Group Captain. Nobody can do anything now. I'm the only man who knows the code.'

Mandrake opened a bottle of the General's rain water. 'How much water, sir?'

'About half and half.'

Mandrake carried the glasses across to Ripper's desk and gave one of them to the General. Ripper smiled and took the drink with his left hand, while he kept his right hand on the gun on his desk.

He lifted his glass and said, 'To peace on earth and to the purity of our bodies.' They touched glasses and both of them drank.

Mandrake looked at the General's relaxed, confident face with a feeling of shock. He could not believe what Ripper had done.

'But General Ripper,' he said, 'you must know that the Russians will retaliate.'

Ripper smiled. 'Now think, Group Captain,' he said. 'The Russians can retaliate only if we don't hit them immediately and with all our strength. And that's exactly what we shall do.'

'I don't understand how you can know that, sir.'

'Group Captain Mandrake,' said General Ripper, 'at this moment, while we sit here and enjoy our conversation, a decision is being made by the President and the military chiefs in the War Room at the Pentagon. When they realize there is no possibility of recalling the bombers, there will be only one thing they can do. They will have to finish the job!'

'Well, I suppose you may be right, General,' said Mandrake.

'Of course I'm right,' Ripper said angrily. He looked at Mandrake strangely. 'Are you a communist, Group Captain?'

'Oh, good lord no, sir,' said Mandrake in a shocked voice. 'I'm an officer of the Royal Air Force.'

'That's what I meant,' said Ripper. 'The RAF is full of Commies – you know that, Group Captain?'

Mandrake was too shocked to reply.

Ripper continued. 'You know, Group Captain, I visited a lot of RAF bases during the Second World War. You know what I saw written on the walls of a lot of them?'

Mandrake shook his head.

'"Joe for King", Group Captain, that's what I saw. And Joe was J. Stalin, Group Captain, remember that – Joseph Stalin.★ And you in the RAF wanted him for king. How do you explain that, if you aren't all Commies?'

'It was just a joke,' said Mandrake. 'You know, people in the Royal Air Force sometimes make strange jokes.'

Ripper suddenly smiled. 'Well, Group Captain, I can understand that. Some people say my jokes are rather strange too.'

★ Joseph Stalin: leader of the USSR from 1922 to 1953.

Chapter 5   Guano Attacks

The War Room

President Muffley had thought carefully about the information he had been given by Turgidson. He made his decision.

'Get Premier* Kissof on the telephone!'

While this was being arranged, General Turgidson stood up again. As he began to speak, he felt confident that the President would have to accept his ideas. He smiled.

'One: we probably won't be able to recall the planes. Two: in less than fifteen minutes, the Russians will see them on their radar. Three: when they do, they will attack us with everything they've got. Four: if we don't do anything to stop them, they will destroy us – probably more than 150 million people will be killed in the United States. Five: if, on the other hand, we *immediately* attack their airports and missile bases, we might be able to stop them.'

General Turgidson smiled confidently at the President, who looked up at him without smiling back.

'General Turgidson,' he said, 'our country has decided never to attack first with nuclear bombs or missiles.'

'Yes,' said General Turgidson, 'but because of what Ripper has done, the Russians are going to attack *us*!'

'We can't be sure of that,' said President Muffley. 'And if we do what you suggest, many of our people will be killed.'

'Well,' said Turgidson, 'I'm not saying that nobody would die, but I don't think it would be more than ten to twenty million.'

'General, you're talking about murder, not war.'

'Mr President, it is necessary to make a choice between losing 20 million people and losing 150 million people.'

* Premier: the leader of a country's government.

The President's headache was getting worse.

'General Turgidson,' he said, 'I think we've heard enough from you.' He looked angrily at the General, who slowly sat down.

A phone began to ring, and the President's assistant picked it up. A few seconds later, he turned to the President.

'Mr President,' he said, 'the Ambassador is waiting upstairs.'

'Bring him down immediately,' said the President.

His assistant spoke quickly into the phone.

General Turgidson stood up again. 'Mr President, are you talking about the *Russian* Ambassador? Are you actually going to let him into the War Room?'

'That is correct, General,' said the President.

'Well, sir,' said Turgidson, 'do you realize how dangerous that could be? I mean, he'll see everything. He'll see the Big Board!'

President Muffley said patiently, 'That's the idea, General.'

Strangelove listened to this and decided, for the moment, to say nothing. Later he would speak, but now he was watching the progress of the bombers on the maps.

Leper Colony

Inside *Leper Colony*, it was time to prepare the bombs. Lieutenant Zogg pressed a switch and a green light came on.

'Ready to begin,' he said.

King felt very satisfied. They had practised this many times, but this time it was real. This was it!

He said happily, 'OK, Dietrich, are you all right?'

Dietrich's voice was calm and confident. 'Right, King.'

The preparation of the bombs needed three men: King, Zogg and Dietrich. This was for safety, so no one person could start a war by mistake.

King said, 'First switch.'

Dietrich repeated this and, at the same time, he and King each pressed a switch in front of them. A second green light came on in front of Zogg. He pressed another switch and a third green light appeared.

He said, 'First switch is ready. Three greens.'

Lieutenant Dietrich had nothing more to do, and he began to play with his radio. King and Zogg continued to prepare the bombs, so they would explode at the correct height. When they had finished, the two men checked everything they had done.

'Check complete,' said Zogg.

'OK, Zogg,' said King, 'check complete.'

Below them, the two bombs waited. The men had given them names: *Hi There!* and *Dear John*. Now they were ready to go.

King was sure they *would* go.

Burpelson Air Force Base

The night was ending and the base was beginning to get light.

Inside the fence, defence teams were waiting. The men on one side of the base heard the sound of vehicles in the distance. They pointed their guns in the direction from which the noise was coming.

'Hey, look!' said one man. 'Eight vehicles, and they're full of soldiers.'

'It must be the Commies,' said another man. 'Who else would come here at four o'clock in the morning?'

'But they look like American vehicles,' said a third man.

'Yeah,' said the second man again, 'these Commies are really clever.'

As the vehicles slowly came closer, the men inside the base waited. Then, when the first vehicle was about two hundred metres away, they began to fire their guns. Immediately, the vehicles stopped and men jumped out from them, running to escape the bullets. The first vehicle exploded and began to burn. In the light of the flames, men could be seen disappearing quickly into the fields on each side of the road. They were experienced soldiers and soon they were attacking the base from all sides.

The commander of the attacking soldiers spoke into his radio, and slowly the guns stopped shooting. In the silence, the noise of the night insects was heard.

Then, behind one of the vehicles, the commanding officer began to speak. He said, his voice loud and clear, 'Men, this is Colonel Guano of the US Army. Why are you firing at us?'

There was silence on the base. Guano waited thirty seconds and then tried again.

'This is Colonel Guano. I repeat, Colonel Guano. We have come from the President. We want to enter the base and speak to General Ripper.'

Again there was no reply, and in the silence some of Guano's men began to move forward. The men in the base began to fire again. Bullets passed close to Colonel Guano and the officers who were with him.

'They must all be crazy!' he said. 'What's happening?'

He thought for a moment, then made his decision. He gave orders to his officers and they went back to their men.

From all sides of the base, the attackers moved forward.

Chapter 6   The Ambassador

Leper Colony

The bomber was down to six thousand metres as it got near to the coast.

Lieutenant Kivel checked his radar and his map, then said,

'We'll cross the coast in about six minutes. Our direction looks good.'

'Thanks,' said King. He looked ahead towards the enemy coast, but he could not see it yet.

Lieutenant Dietrich, the defence officer, was also looking at his radar, but he was looking for enemy missiles and fighter planes.

Suddenly, Dietrich saw something. He watched it carefully, then said, 'Missile! One hundred kilometres away, coming in fast.'

King said calmly, 'All right.' He thought about what he should do. They were still too high to escape the missile, and they were not going to get down to a safe height before the missile arrived. 'Dietrich, can you see any fighter planes on the radar?'

'No', said Dietrich, 'just the missile. It's seventy kilometres away now.'

King thought about the situation again.

'Sixty,' said Dietrich. 'It's still coming!'

King made his decision. 'Prepare to drop Quail.'

Lieutenant Zogg pressed a few switches and made some checks. He said, 'Quail ready to go.'

'Open bomb doors.'

Zogg said immediately, 'Bomb doors are open.'

King waited. The Quail was a special missile. Its purpose was to lead enemy missiles away from the bomber. *Leper Colony* carried only one Quail, so the decision to use it was very important.

'Fifty!' said Dietrich.

King decided. 'Drop Quail,' he said calmly.

The Quail dropped out of the bomber and fell for a few metres. Then a jet flame appeared as it came to life.

King turned the bomber to a new direction. 'Close bomb doors,' he said.

Zogg said, 'Bomb doors closed.'

Dietrich's voice was high and excited. 'Thirty kilometres, coming in straight.'

King continued to turn the bomber, but below it the Quail turned in the same direction.

Zogg looked at his radar. He said quickly, 'Something must be wrong. Quail turned with us.'

Immediately, King began to turn the plane in the opposite direction.

'Twenty-five!' said Dietrich.

Again the Quail turned with the bomber. It was only about a hundred metres below them.

'It's still following us,' said Zogg.

'Fifteen!'

'Hold on, boys,' said King, and he turned the plane violently to get away from Quail.

'Ten kilometres!' said Dietrich.

King suddenly made the plane climb as steeply as he could. Captain Ace Owens turned the engine power up.

Zogg said, 'It's still with us. Following like a dog.'

'Five kilometres!' said Dietrich.

The Russian missile was still climbing when it got near *Leper Colony*. It hit the Quail one hundred metres below the bomber, and there was a big explosion.

The bomber jumped violently. It filled with smoke as King tried to control it.

'I think we've been hit,' he said. 'I'm taking her down.'

As the plane moved down towards the enemy coast, King asked for damage reports from the other men. Only one man did not reply. Ace Owens looked at King and opened his mouth to make a word. But the word did not come. His eyes closed and he fell back in his seat.

On the main map, the bombers could be seen moving forward. The Russian Ambassador watched them and then said angrily, 'You are very clever, Mr President! You send nuclear planes to destroy Russia! You call me in here and tell me the planes are coming but that it is an *accident*. You say, "Do not retaliate, Russia, this is an accident." Ha! You are clever, Mr President, but we are not stupid.'

President Muffley looked at Ambassador De Sadeski for a moment. He had known him for several years and he also knew that De Sadeski was friendly with the most powerful people in the USSR.

'Mr Ambassador,' he said, 'you're a very intelligent man. You must understand that there is only one way we can escape this disaster. When I speak to the Premier, it's important that he believes me. You'll be able to tell him that what I say is true. That's why I brought you here.'

An assistant filled some glasses from a bottle of vodka and offered a glass to De Sadeski.

'Here you are, sir.'

De Sadeski took the glass, lifted it to his lips, then suddenly put it down on the table. He looked at the President and said slowly, 'Have you put anything in this?'

The President did not answer. He took another glass and quickly drank the vodka.

De Sadeski said, 'I'm sorry, but you will understand that I have to be very careful.'

'Perhaps you'll now accept that what I'm saying is true,' said President Muffley.

De Sadeski said nothing, but he took another glass and drank the vodka like water.

'Mmm. Good,' he said.

The President relaxed in his chair. He said quietly, 'Won't you have something to eat now? You must be feeling hungry and we may have a long wait down here.'

The Ambassador looked at the long table, which was covered in food. He was feeling hungry.

'OK,' he said.

De Sadeski followed the President's assistant to the table and looked carefully at all the food. He could only find one kind of food that was not there. He asked for it.

'Don't you have any fresh fish?'

The assistant was embarrassed. He looked quickly along the table.

'I'm afraid not, sir.'

De Sadeski felt pleased. Now he could relax a little.

He said, 'I'll have some eggs, then. And bring me some cigars – Cuban, of course.'

The President said, 'Why is that phone call to Premier Kissof taking so long?'

His assistant replied, 'Mr President, we haven't been able to speak to him. They say they don't know where he is.'

De Sadeski said, 'Are you having problems reaching the Premier?'

'Yes, we are, Ambassador.'

'On Saturday afternoon his office will not know where to find him. Try Moscow 87-46-56.'

'Thank you very much, Ambassador,' said the President.

De Sadeski smiled. 'Our Premier is a man of the people, but he is also . . . a *man*, if you understand me.'

President Muffley laughed. 'Fine,' he said.

General Turgidson was angry that the President was being so friendly to the Ambassador.

'Dirty Commie!' he said to another officer.

De Sadeski heard him. He said to the President, 'I formally

request that you have this fool sent out of the War Room.'

President Muffley turned to Turgidson and said, 'General, the Russian Ambassador is here as my guest. You must be polite to him. You understand me?'

Turgidson's face was red with anger, but he said, 'Yes, Mr President.'

The President's assistant said, 'Mr President, I think they're trying the phone number.'

The President stood up and walked towards his assistant. Suddenly, he heard a noise behind him. General Turgidson and Ambassador De Sadeski were fighting on the floor, crashing into tables and chairs.

President Muffley turned and shouted, 'Gentlemen! For the love of God! What are you doing?'

Some officers held the two men away from each other.

General Buck Turgidson said, 'You dirty Commie, I'll knock that Commie head off your Commie neck.'

President Muffley stepped between the two men.

De Sadeski said, 'Mr President, my government will hear of this personal attack.'

President Muffley said, 'Gentlemen, I want an explanation!'

De Sadeski pointed. 'You will find an explanation in the right hand of this violent fool.'

Turgidson smiled. 'That's right, Mr Commie. Here is the explanation, Mr President!'

He opened his hand and showed the President a very small spy camera.

'This Commie rat was using this to take pictures of the Big Board!'

Ambassador De Sadeski said, 'Mr President, this fool tried to put that camera in my coat pocket, but I stopped him.'

'That's a lie!' shouted Turgidson. 'I saw him with my own eyes.'

President Muffley said, 'Now stop this. Gentlemen, this has gone too far. You will stop it immediately.'

The President's assistant saved the situation. He said in an excited voice, 'Mr President, I think they're getting the Premier.'

Chapter 7   Pure Water

Leper Colony

King looked closely at Ace and shouted, 'Hey, one of you come and look at Ace here.'

Dietrich left his seat and moved forward.

King checked his instruments. There were fire-warning lights on engines three and four. He said, 'I'm shutting down three and four,' and he pressed the switches.

As the fuel to the engines was cut, the fire died. The smoke was still thick inside the plane, and King knew they had to get down to a low level as fast as possible.

'I'm taking her down,' he said, 'very low. Is that OK, Kivel?'

Kivel looked at his map. 'Yes, King, there's no high ground yet.'

The bomber started to go down. Dietrich, who was trying to get Ace out of his seat, said, 'I can't move him while we're going down. King, it looks like he's hit in the shoulder.'

King said, 'Zogg, have you got any damage?'

'No damage, King.'

'All right, come up here and help.'

Zogg climbed up and helped Dietrich to move Ace Owens to a bed at the back of the plane.

King saw that his instruments were normal, and then asked his men for damage reports.

Kivel said, 'Everything's working fine, but there's one little thing I'm worried about.'

'What's that?'

'I think we may be losing fuel.'

'Well, we're still flying,' said King. 'That's what's important. What about you, Goldberg?'

Lieutenant Goldberg's voice was excited. He said, 'Well, King, I haven't finished my check yet. But there's a big hole in the side of the plane opposite the radio. I'm checking it now.'

'OK,' said King. He made himself more comfortable in his seat and watched for the enemy coast. There were many dangers ahead, he knew: high ground which was not shown on the maps, fighter planes, ground-to-air missiles. But he knew that the enemy would not be able to see them on their radar if they were flying fast and near the ground.

He said, 'We're going to fly as fast as possible at ground level.'

Kivel replied immediately. 'We'll use a lot of fuel.'

'We've got no choice,' said King. 'What about the wind?'

'It's behind us, so it'll help us now,' said Kivel, 'but we'll have problems when we turn round to go back home.'

'Well,' said King, 'we'll worry about that when the time comes.'

He looked ahead and saw the enemy coast.

Burpelson Air Force Base

Ripper's office had been badly damaged in the fighting. Ripper and Mandrake were sitting on the floor behind the General's desk. Their glasses were beside them on the carpet, and Ripper was holding a machine gun across his knees.

Ripper smiled as he listened to the noise of the fighting out on the base.

He said, 'The boys are doing well, Group Captain.'

'Yes,' said Mandrake, 'they certainly are.'

Ripper drank slowly from his glass and said, 'Group Captain Mandrake, have you ever seen a Russian drink a glass of water?'

'No, sir, I don't believe I ever have.'

'Vodka. That's what they drink, isn't it? Never water.'

'Well, I – I don't really know, sir.'

'A Russian never drinks water, and there's a good reason for that.'

Mandrake looked at Ripper anxiously. He could not understand what he was talking about. But Ripper seemed to be perfectly calm.

Mandrake said, 'I'm afraid I don't quite understand what you're saying.'

Ripper took his cigar out of his mouth and said, 'Water! That's what I'm saying, *water!* All life comes from water. Four-fifths of the earth is covered in water. Most of the human body is water. We need fresh, pure water to keep our bodies pure. Are you beginning to understand, Group Captain?'

'No, sir, I'm afraid I'm not.'

'Have you never wondered why I only drink rain water and only pure alcohol?'

Mandrake said, 'Yes, sir, I have wondered – yes.'

Ripper looked at his empty glass. He gave it to Mandrake, who crossed the floor on his knees and filled it up again.

Ripper said, 'Have you ever heard of a thing called fluoride, Group Captain?'

Mandrake paused to think about the question, then replied, 'Yes, I think so, sir. Don't they add fluoride to water to protect our teeth?'

Just then, there was a sound of shooting outside the window and more bullets hit the wall of the office.

The General said, 'That sounded close. Help me with this gun.'

He stood up and walked towards the window, carrying the gun, while Mandrake went forward on his knees, holding the belt of bullets.

The General immediately saw a man with a gun on the

building opposite the office. He began to fire the heavy machine gun, which jumped in his hands and made a lot of noise. Soon the carpet was covered with empty bullet cases.

Ripper stopped for a moment, stared out through the broken windows and then fired again. He stopped and said to Mandrake in a satisfied voice, 'That's done it. I got him.'

They both sat down on the floor and Ripper picked up his glass again.

'As I was saying,' he said, 'fluoridation of water is the communists' most dangerous secret plan. Fluorides are poisons. They are used to kill rats! They destroy the purity of our bodies!'

Mandrake said thoughtfully, 'Well, sir, I think the scientists have checked it. That's what I've read.'

Ripper smiled. 'Exactly, Group Captain. That just shows how powerful the communists are – you only have to count the number of scientists and politicians who support fluoridation. *The facts are all there*, Group Captain! Do you know any facts about fluorides, Group Captain Mandrake?'

Mandrake felt his moustache. He said, 'Well, no, sir.'

Outside, the sound of guns was getting louder and closer.

Ripper touched Mandrake on the shoulder. 'You're a good officer, Group Captain,' he said. 'In future, don't call me sir. Call me Jack. That's an order.'

Mandrake felt uncomfortable. Things like this did not happen in the Royal Air Force. He drank from his glass and said, 'I understand . . . Jack.'

Ripper listened to the sound of the shooting outside, then said, 'Those are my boys out there. They're fighting. They're dying for me, you know that.'

'And I'm sure they're very proud and pleased to do it,' Mandrake said enthusiastically.

'I'm glad to hear you say that,' Ripper said. 'What were we talking about?'

'Well, you were asking me if I knew any facts about fluorides.'

'Well,' said Ripper, 'did you know that in addition to fluoridating water, they are planning to fluoridate salt, fruit juices, soup, sugar, milk and ice cream! *Ice cream*, Group Captain. *Children's* ice cream! Do you know when fluoridation first began, Group Captain?'

'No, I don't think I do, Jack.'

Ripper took his cigar out of his mouth and looked at it carefully. He said slowly, 'It began in 1946. Do you understand now?'

'Well . . .' said Mandrake.

Ripper continued. 'It was 1946, Group Captain. Immediately after the Second World War. That's when the communists started to put this poison into our bodies without our knowledge or choice. That's the way the Commies work.'

'Jack,' said Mandrake, 'when did you first think of this idea?'

'It's *not* an idea,' said Ripper. 'It's a certain fact.'

'Yes, I see that, Jack, but when did you first realize it?'

Ripper looked at Mandrake. Slowly he said, 'Have you ever loved a woman, Group Captain? Physically loved her? Afterwards you feel tired and empty. Luckily, I understood what this meant: I had lost my power. But I can tell you that it has never happened again, Group Captain. Women want my power, but I don't give it to them.'

Mandrake did not know what to say to the General, who was looking at the wall. But he realized that the fighting had stopped and that the base was now silent.

Ripper realized it too. He crossed to the window and looked out. In the distance he saw a group of his men standing without guns and with their hands on their heads. He turned away from the window. His face suddenly looked old.

He said, 'They've failed.'

Chapter 8   An Important Phone Call

Leper Colony

The bomber was now flying very low. King looked out and saw snow on the ground and high mountains on both sides.

Goldberg left his seat and went forward to Ace's bed. Ace looked up at him.

'How are you doing, Goldberg?'

'I'm fine,' said Goldberg. 'And you, Ace?'

'I'm OK,' said Ace. He closed his eyes.

When Goldberg got back to his seat, he spoke to King.

'King, I just looked at Ace. He doesn't look very good. But I think he'll live.'

'Well, that's good,' said King.

'But, King,' said Goldberg, 'the radio's broken and I can't repair it.'

The War Room

All the people in the War Room suddenly stopped talking. They heard the President's assistant say, 'Mr President, they've got the Premier on the phone. His translator is with him, so you can speak to him.'

The President took the phone. Around the table the group quickly sat down, and twenty-three hands picked up twenty-three phones.

The President said, 'Hello? Hello? Dimitri, is that you?' He paused for the answer, then continued, 'Yes, this is Merkin, how are you? . . . Oh, fine, just fine, thank you. Listen, I'm very sorry to phone you at this number . . . Oh, yes, the Ambassador gave it to me . . . Yes, he's here with me now. I've got a problem that I've got to talk to you about. But first I want him to say hello to you.'

The President covered the telephone with his hand and said quietly to De Sadeski, 'Tell him where you are and that you will enter the conversation if I say anything that's not true. But please don't say any more than that.'

De Sadeski took another phone and started to speak in Russian. When he had finished, he waited for the reply. Then he said to the President, 'Be careful, Mr President. I think he's drunk.'

The President spoke into his phone again. 'Hello? Yes, it's me again, Dimitri. What? I can't hear you very well. Do you think they could turn that music down? Thanks, that's much better.'

He wondered exactly what to say. He laughed nervously.

'Now, Dimitri, you know how we've always talked about the possibility of something going wrong with the bomb? . . . The bomb, Dimitri, you know, the *nuclear* bomb . . . Well, what happened is this. One of our base commanders went a little strange in the head. And he did a silly thing. Well, he ordered his planes to attack your country.'

The President held the phone away from his ear.

'Yes, but . . .' he said, 'let me finish, Dimitri . . . let me finish . . . *let me finish*! That's right, thirty-four planes, but they won't reach their targets for another hour . . . Well, listen, how do you think I feel about it? Why do you think I'm calling you? . . . Yes, I've talked to the Ambassador about this. We've been trying to recall them but there's a problem about the code . . . All right, I'll listen to you.'

The President looked at his assistant, who put a cigarette between the President's lips. The President breathed in deeply and blew out a cloud of smoke. His hand was shaking as the voice of the Premier finished.

The President said, 'What are you talking about? This doesn't have to be the end of the world. Don't talk like that, Dimitri.'

Turgidson smiled. He liked the way the conversation was going.

The President interrupted the Premier. He said loudly, 'Listen, Dimitri, we're wasting time. We'd like to give you full information about the targets and the flight plans of the planes ... That's right, if we can't recall the planes, then, well, we're just going to have to help you destroy them, Dimitri. But who should we call?'

He began to write quickly. As he wrote, he repeated the information the Russian Premier was giving him.

'The People's Central Air Defence Centre. Where is that, Dimitri? ... In Omsk. Right. You call them first ... OK, I've got the number ... OK, goodbye.'

The President covered his phone again and turned to the Ambassador.

'He wants to talk to you.'

Ambassador De Sadeski began to talk quickly in Russian. Suddenly he became silent, then asked a few questions, then put the phone down.

The President looked at him anxiously.

'What happened?'

De Sadeski said quietly, 'The fools! The mad, crazy fools!'

The President said quickly, 'What are you talking about?'

'The Doomsday Machine.'

Around the table men turned to each other, repeating De Sadeski's words. None of them knew what he was talking about.

De Sadeski spoke quietly.

'The Doomsday Machine. It will destroy all human and animal life on earth.' He suddenly began to talk in Russian.

Nobody understood what he was saying, but they realized from his voice that something terrible had happened.

Dr Strangelove understood. He began to think of a plan, but for the moment he said nothing.

Chapter 9   The Doomsday Machine

Leper Colony

Kivel was checking his computer. He looked worried.

Zogg looked at him and said, 'Is something wrong?'

'Well, it looks bad,' Kivel said. 'Hey, King, we're using a lot of fuel.'

'Yes,' said King, 'we use a lot when we're flying low.'

Kivel shook his head. 'Yes, I know. But we're using a lot more than we should.'

King laughed. 'Check again. You navigators always make mistakes.'

Dietrich went to see Ace.

'Can I get you anything, Ace?' he said. 'Coffee or something?'

'I'd like some water,' said Ace. 'My throat seems dry.'

Dietrich filled a paper cup with water and gave it to Ace, who drank it thirstily.

'Now, you try to get some sleep,' said Dietrich. Ace closed his eyes. Dietrich watched him for a few seconds and then went back to his seat.

Kivel checked the numbers again and then passed them to Zogg to check. Zogg looked at them for a minute and then said, 'I can't see any mistakes.'

Kivel said, 'King, I was right. We're using twice as much fuel as we should.'

King said quickly, 'But we've got enough to get to our first target?'

'Yes.'

'And the second?'

'Well yes, but we'll have to walk home.'

'They've failed,' Ripper repeated. His voice sounded angry and hurt.

Mandrake put a hand on his elbow.

He said, 'They did their best, Jack. They couldn't win.'

'They were my boys,' said Ripper, 'and they failed.'

'It doesn't matter, Jack,' said Mandrake. He came close and spoke to Ripper urgently. 'Jack, just give me the recall code – we don't have much time now. Give me the code, then everything will be all right.'

Ripper looked at Mandrake, but his eyes did not see him. His voice was dead.

'It can't ever be all right for me again, not after what's happened.'

'Don't talk like that, Jack,' said Mandrake quickly. 'Just give me the code, and then I'll look after you. You need a rest. They'll put you in a nice hospital. Jack, please give me the code.'

Ripper said, '"Joe for King," Group Captain, that's what they had written on the walls. Well, let me tell you something, Joe's never going to be king. Joe's dead, Group Captain.'

Ripper stood up and began to walk slowly across the office. At the door he paused.

He turned and said, 'I'm going for a walk, Group Captain. Remember the purity of your body, and remember "Joe for King".' Then he went through the door and shut it behind him.

For a moment, Mandrake did not move. Then he went quickly to the door and ran outside. He could not see Ripper anywhere. He looked for him for several minutes but could not find him. Then he returned to the office.

In a room behind the War Room, Air Force officers were sending radio messages to Russia. They were giving information about the attacking bombers: their exact heights and speeds, their targets, how much fuel they had, and how many defence missiles they were carrying.

In the War Room, there was silence as everyone thought about what the Russian Ambassador had said. They all looked at him.

De Sadeski said slowly, 'A Doomsday Machine, gentlemen. It is such a large nuclear bomb that, twelve months after it explodes, the earth will be as dead as the moon. And no life will be possible on earth for another ninety-three years.'

'Mr Ambassador,' said the President, 'I'm afraid I don't understand. Does the Premier say that he will explode this if our planes succeed in their attack?'

'No, sir,' said De Sadeski. 'Only a mad man would do that. The Doomsday Machine will explode *automatically*!'

'But the Premier can stop it, can't he?'

'No! If anybody tries to stop it, it will explode.'

General Turgidson laughed. He turned to the colonel beside him and said quietly, 'It's a Commie lie.' He looked at the President. 'And *he* sits there wasting time.'

The President was confused. 'But surely, Ambassador, this is madness. Why did you build it?'

De Sadeski said, 'Some of us fought against it, but in the end we could not stay in the race against the US. Our bombs were not big enough. Our people wanted more food and clothes. The Doomsday Machine cost us much less than what we were spending on nuclear defence every year. We also learned that your country was building a similar thing, and we were afraid.'

'That's crazy!' said the President. 'I've never agreed to anything like that.'

'We read it in the *New York Times*.'

President Muffley turned to Dr Strangelove. 'Do we have anything like this?'

'Mr President,' said Dr Strangelove, 'I ordered a study of this idea last year. After reading the report, I decided that it was not a sensible idea. Now you can see why.'

President Muffley looked very tired.

'You mean it's possible that they have built this thing? Really possible?'

The Russian Ambassador spoke. 'It's not difficult, Mr President.'

'But,' said Muffley, 'is it really possible for it to explode automatically, and at the same time for it to be impossible to stop?'

Dr Strangelove said, 'Mr President, it is not only possible, it is necessary. That is the idea of this machine. It is important to make the enemy afraid to attack. That is exactly what the Doomsday Machine can do.' He turned to look at De Sadeski. 'There is only one thing I don't understand, Mr Ambassador. The Doomsday Machine cannot frighten the enemy if it is a secret. Why didn't you tell the world?'

De Sadeski turned away.

He said quietly, 'The Premier was going to make it public on Monday. As you know, he loves surprises.'

Just then, General Faceman interrupted. He had just been given a message. 'Excuse me, sir. The base at Burpelson has been taken.'

The President felt a little hope.

He said, 'Have you got the commanding general on the phone?'

'We will in a minute, sir.'

38

Chapter 10   The Recall Code

Burpelson Air Force Base

Group Captain Mandrake was standing by Ripper's desk. He picked up a piece of paper on which Ripper had written *Joe for King* several times. He began to have an idea.

He did not notice an army officer who walked quietly into the room with his gun held forward ready to shoot. This was Colonel Guano, the commander of the soldiers who had attacked Burpelson.

Mandrake was talking to himself.

'Joe for King. Hmm. JFK ... FJK ... KFJ.'

Guano looked at him and said, 'OK, soldier, put your hands on your head.'

Mandrake did not seem to notice him until Colonel Guano fired two bullets into the desk. Mandrake jumped with shock and quickly put his hands up.

'Quickly! Quickly!' said Guano. 'Hands on head, soldier. What kind of suit is that?'

'It's not a suit, it's the uniform of the Royal Air Force,' said Mandrake. 'I am Group Captain Lionel Mandrake, General Ripper's assistant.'

'*Keep your hands up!* Where's General Ripper?'

'Well, I'm afraid General Ripper's disappeared.' Mandrake laughed nervously. 'He just ran out. What a pity you missed him.'

Guano moved across to the open door of the office, but he kept his gun pointing at Mandrake. He looked outside, but there was nobody there.

'So he just ran out, did he?'

'That's right,' said Mandrake quickly. 'Now listen, Colonel, I think I know what the recall code is. I must contact the Pentagon.' He began to move towards the phone.

'Just keep your hands on your head, Group Captain.'

Mandrake tried to stay calm. He said, 'Colonel, we must hurry. You see, I think it's connected with "Joe for King". It could be JFK ... FJK ... JKF ... KJF ... KFJ.' His voice died as Guano pushed his gun at him.

Guano was beginning to feel that he was in a room with a madman. Mandrake's long hair and strange uniform made this feeling stronger. He tried to speak in a friendly voice.

'Sure. Now just keep your hands on the top of your head, and let's start walking out of here. OK?'

Mandrake said quickly, 'Colonel, don't you know what's happened?'

'Now, just keep calm and start walking.'

'You don't understand, do you, Colonel? Don't you know that General Ripper went mad? He sent all his planes to attack Russia!'

Guano looked at Mandrake. He knew there must be a reason why he had been ordered to attack the base, but he couldn't believe what Mandrake was saying.

He said, 'Now, don't get excited.'

Mandrake said, 'Colonel, if we don't hurry, the whole world may be destroyed.'

Guano stepped back. Mandrake looked at him carefully. He thought he could see a feeling of doubt in the Colonel's face.

'Now please,' he said quickly, 'just let me pick up this nice red telephone. See.'

He moved forward to the phone and spoke to Guano like a child.

'Now, you see, I'm picking up the phone, slowly, OK?' He spoke into the phone. 'Hello? Hello? ... Oh no, it's dead.'

Colonel Guano was watching him carefully.

Mandrake said, 'Now see, I'm picking up this other

telephone . . . It's dead too. It was that stupid fighting.' He put the telephone down angrily.

Guano said quietly, 'Now listen to me. You've wasted enough of my time. Start walking.'

Mandrake began to walk out of the office. Guano followed him, with his gun in Mandrake's back.

Mandrake said, 'Colonel, what exactly do you think has been happening here this morning?'

'My orders didn't say anything about planes attacking Russia,' said Guano. 'I was only told to put General Ripper on the phone with the President of the United States.'

'Of course!' said Mandrake. He stopped and turned to look at Guano. His voice was excited now. 'You said the President wants to speak to General Ripper, didn't you? Well, Ripper's not here, is he? And I'm his assistant, so he'll want to speak to me.' He pointed to a pay phone near them. 'Let me try that phone.'

Guano looked at Mandrake. 'You want to talk to the President? You?' He laughed.

Mandrake's voice was quiet but strong. 'Colonel, if the Pentagon hears that you stopped me phoning, you'll be lucky if they let you wear the uniform of a toilet cleaner.'

Guano thought for a few moments. Then he said slowly, 'OK, try and phone the President of the United States.'

Mandrake ran to the phone. He put his hand in his pocket and pulled out some money. It was not enough.

'Colonel,' he said. 'I need fifty cents.'

'I don't carry coins when I'm fighting,' said Guano.

Mandrake was upset. Then he saw a Coca-Cola machine behind the Colonel. Suddenly, there was hope.

He said, 'Colonel, I want you to shoot the lock off that Coca-Cola machine. There must be a lot of money in there.'

'That's private property, Group Captain,' said Guano.

Mandrake said, 'Colonel, just imagine what will happen to

your job when they learn that you didn't help me. Shoot it, man! That's what bullets are for.'

Guano could hear the urgency in Mandrake's voice. He turned and carefully fired two bullets into the coin box of the Coca-Cola machine. Coins poured out on to the floor.

And Coca-Cola poured out into the Colonel's face.

As he tried to clean his face, the Colonel heard Mandrake speaking into the phone.

'I have to talk to the President ... It's Grou ... No, it's Burpelson Air Force Base ... You'll find he wants to talk to us ... All right, I'll wait, but please hurry!'

Guano listened with surprise.

Mandrake heard a man's voice.

'This is General Faceman's assistant. Is that Burpelson?'

'Yes,' said Mandrake, 'but I want the President.'

'You can give your message to me,' said the voice.

Mandrake thought for a moment. He looked at his watch and saw that the bombers must now be close to their targets.

'All right, but please remember that this is very urgent.'

'Don't worry,' said the voice. 'What's the message?'

'Well,' said Mandrake, 'you know General Ripper went completely mad and sent all his bombers against Russia?'

'Yes, we do.'

'Well, I think the recall code is JFK, from "Joe for King".'

'Joe King? Who's he?'

'Not Joe King,' shouted Mandrake. 'Joe *for* King. Oh, it's not important. Just remember JFK.'

'OK,' said the voice. 'JFK. I'll tell them.'

Mandrake put the phone down.

Guano said, 'Did you get him? Did you speak to the President?'

'No,' said Mandrake, 'I spoke to General Faceman's assistant.'

'OK,' said Guano. 'Well, maybe I was wrong about you, but now let's go and find General Ripper.'

'Just a moment,' said Mandrake. 'I need to go back to my office to get my hat.'

'OK,' said Guano, 'but be quick.'

As they walked into Mandrake's office, the telephone rang. Mandrake looked at it in surprise. Then he picked it up and said, 'Yes, this is Group Captain Mandrake. In what? . . . Five minutes ago. I see.'

He put the phone down and turned to Guano.

'I don't think we'll find General Ripper, Colonel.'

'Why not?' asked Guano.

'Because,' said Mandrake slowly, 'he just took off in his personal plane. And he's not only mad, he's also very drunk!'

Chapter 11   Flying Low

The War Room

In the War Room, everyone was looking at the map of Russia. While they watched, they saw their planes turn round as they heard the recall code. Every time they saw a plane change its direction on the map, the men round the table shouted happily.

The President looked across the table at General Faceman.

'What was the name of the officer who called me from Burpelson?'

Faceman said, 'I didn't speak to him, sir. But Colonel Guano was leading the attack, so *he* probably made the call.'

'I want that officer to be made a general.'

'Yes, sir.'

The President turned to Turgidson.

'Let me know when all the planes have received the recall code.'

'Almost all of them have, now,' said Turgidson quickly.

43

'How many planes did we lose?' asked the President.

'We're not certain, sir. We think the Russians destroyed four planes.'

'I see.'

Suddenly General Turgidson climbed on a chair and asked for silence.

'Gentlemen,' he said in a serious voice, 'I want to suggest that we get down on our knees and thank God that we have been saved.'

Soon everyone in the room was on their knees except for De Sadeski and Dr Strangelove. De Sadeski looked round the room and said, 'Excuse me, but I'm afraid I have much more urgent things to do.'

Men looked at him with shock and anger.

De Sadeski continued. 'But before I leave, I want to say that it will not be enough to satisfy my government if you apologize for this shocking attack on the peace-loving people of the USSR.'

The President stood up and looked angrily at De Sadeski.

'You know that this was done by a madman! We're not responsible.'

De Sadeski said, 'It is very convenient for you to blame someone who is not here.'

The President was getting very angry now.

'I've warned your country about this danger for years, but you didn't listen.'

'You never wanted to destroy your bombs,' said De Sadeski. 'It would destroy your economy.'

'That's not true! We could spend the same amount of money on schools, roads and space travel.'

De Sadeski was also becoming angry. 'You only wanted to spy on our country.'

'You know that's a lie, De Sadeski,' said the President. 'We couldn't destroy *our* bombs when we didn't know what you were doing inside your country!'

'And we, Mr President, could not let you spy in our country before you destroyed your bombs.'

The President said nothing for several seconds. Then he continued, in a quieter voice, 'Nations have always behaved badly, and now the Bomb has become an even greater enemy to every nation than those nations have ever been or could be to each other. And we can never completely destroy the Bomb because now we will always have the knowledge of how to make it.'

De Sadeski was going to reply, but just then the President's assistant interrupted.

'Mr President, Premier Kissof is calling again.'

The President looked again at De Sadeski, then picked up the phone.

Leper Colony

Leper Colony was only a few metres above the snowy ground. King smiled as he turned into a valley between two big hills. This was *real* flying.

Kivel said, 'King, we're still using too much fuel down here. It's going to be a long walk after we hit our first target.'

Lieutenant Goldberg said, 'OK, so we walk.'

Dietrich said, 'I can walk.' He moved forward to look at Ace Owens.

Zogg said, 'Well, a walk is a walk is a walk.'

Dietrich looked at Ace. He had already given him some medicine and now he was sleeping.

Goldberg said, 'King, the radio is definitely broken. I can't repair it.'

'OK, Goldberg, so forget about it,' King said calmly.

'Forget about it?' said Goldberg.

'Sure,' said King. 'What do they need to talk to us about now?'

Kivel said, 'Can't we go higher, King? We'd use less fuel.'

King turned the plane again as a hill came up in front. Then he said, 'Listen, Kivel. If we stay low, their radar probably won't find us and we should get to the first target. Then we'll fly towards the coast and jump out when the fuel's finished.'

'Well,' said Kivel, 'if it's OK with you, King, then it's OK with me.'

Dietrich had gone back to his seat and was looking closely at his radar.

'King,' he said urgently, 'I think there are four fighter planes coming.'

'Are you sure?' asked King.

'I'm sure,' said Dietrich. 'They're flying lower, and they're only thirty kilometres away now.'

'Prepare to fire missiles.'

'How many, King?'

'As many as you think you need.'

'OK,' said Dietrich. 'Goldberg, prepare missiles one to eight.'

Goldberg quickly pressed some switches in front of him. He said, 'One to eight ready.'

Dietrich looked at the radar, waited a moment, then said, 'Fire missiles!'

Lieutenant Goldberg pressed the button.

The missiles left the tail of the bomber, and Dietrich and Goldberg watched them on their radar as they moved towards the attacking fighters. One by one the missiles reached the fighters, and the fighters disappeared.

'Got them!' said Dietrich.

'Got them *all*!' said Goldberg.

Suddenly, they felt an explosion in *Leper Colony*.

'What was that?' said King, as the plane filled with smoke again.

Goldberg said, 'I think one of those fighters fired a missile before it was hit.'

'How's Ace?'

'Still asleep.'

'Check on damage.'

Zogg said, 'We've got another hole in the side.'

'Equipment?'

'Seems OK.'

Kivel said, 'We've lost more fuel, King. I don't know what the answer is now.'

'I'll find one,' said King.

Dietrich suddenly said, 'King, Ace is dead.'

'What do you mean, he's dead?'

Dietrich's voice was quiet. 'He's dead, King, that's all.'

'He was a good man,' said King, 'but that's war.'

Goldberg helped Dietrich to close Ace Owens's eyes and to cover him with a blanket.

'Yes,' he said, 'that's war.'

Chapter 12   A New Target

The War Room

Everyone sitting round the big table listened carefully as President Muffley spoke to the Russian Premier.

He said, 'Hello? Premier Kissof? That's right, it's Merkin.' He paused. 'Oh no, there must be a mistake. Just a second.' He looked at General Turgidson. 'Kissof says one plane is still attacking. They think its target might be Laputa.'

General Turgidson smiled. 'Well, that's impossible, Mr President. Look at the Big Board. Thirty-four planes attacking, thirty recalled, four destroyed. One of those four was going to Laputa.'

President Muffley said into his phone, 'Hello, Dimitri? Yes, well, all the planes have been recalled except for the four you destroyed ... What do you mean, *three*? ... You mean it's only damaged and it's still coming in? ... I see. Just wait a second, will you?' He looked again at Turgidson.

Turgidson was looking at the Big Board. There were now more than 500 Russian planes flying towards the US.

He said, 'Mr President, I think the Commies are lying about that fourth plane. They just want a reason to attack us.'

The President shook his head and looked up at the map of Russia. Only one US plane was shown now. It was still moving towards its target.

The President talked into his telephone again. 'Hello? ... Listen, Dimitri, if this report is true, and if you can't destroy the plane before it bombs its target, what will happen? Will the Doomsday Machine explode? ... Are you sure? ... OK, we'll just have to stop that plane.'

He gave the phone to his assistant and spoke to General Turgidson.

'Is there really a chance for that plane to reach its target?'

'Well, sir,' said Turgidson, 'if the pilot's a good man, he can fly that plane really low.' He was becoming excited now. This was something he knew a lot about. 'A really big plane, flying so low that it almost touches the ground ...'

'Does he have a chance?' the President said quickly.

'Does he have a chance?' said Turgidson loudly. 'Yes! An *excellent* chance!' He looked round the table. As he saw the unhappy faces of the men there, he suddenly realized what this meant.

The President looked at the maps, then said, 'Now, wait a minute. I think I might have an idea how to get the recall code to them.'

He picked up the phone. 'Well, Dimitri, you're just going to have to stop that plane. I'm sorry they're flying below your radar, but that's their job. Listen, Dimitri, you know exactly where they're going ... yes, Laputa and then Borchav. I'm sure your air defence can find and destroy a single plane ... Just keep calm, Dimitri. We've got to work together on this.'

The President lit a cigarette as he listened to the Russian Premier. Then he said angrily, 'Dimitri, *I* didn't do it, it wasn't me ... Dimitri, all right, he *was* one of our generals, but it isn't going to help us if we argue about that now. Listen, Dimitri, I've got a great idea ... Well, do you want to hear it? OK, why don't you use lights to send the recall code to the plane? Our boys will see it and turn round.'

Dr Strangelove looked at the President as he put the phone down. He did not think those fools would ever succeed in destroying the last plane. He looked away and thought about his plan to save at least a few people.

Leper Colony

King said, 'Kivel, how far can we go on our fuel?'

'Two hundred kilometres,' said Kivel.

'OK,' said King, 'we're not going to get to our first target. Are there any other targets near here?'

Kivel looked at his map and then said, 'There's one called Missile Base 69. It's one hundred and forty kilometres from here.'

'What direction?'

'Two-eight-zero,' said Kivel.

'Two-eight-zero,' King repeated as he turned the plane. Then he said, 'Goldberg, send a message to say that we're going to hit Missile Base 69 instead of Laputa.'

'I can't, King,' Goldberg said quickly.

'Why not?'

'I told you, the radio's not working.'

'OK,' said King calmly. 'It doesn't matter much. Zogg, open

49

the bomb doors when Kivel says we're one hundred and twenty kilometres from the target.'

'Sure, King.'

Chapter 13   Trouble with the Doors

The War Room

'Sir,' said the President's assistant urgently. 'Premier Kissof is on the phone again.'

The President quickly lifted his phone. He said, 'Hello, Dimitri. You did what? How did that happen? . . . Well, hold on a minute, will you?'

He turned to General Turgidson and said, 'They say they've lost the bomber.'

'Mr President, you don't surprise me,' said Turgidson. 'I told you that those boys would be very difficult to follow if they were flying low.'

The President said, 'Hello, Dimitri, are you still there? . . . Yes, well, we knew it was going to be difficult, Dimitri, but there's still a chance we can stop it.'

The Big Board still showed *Leper Colony* flying towards Laputa.

The President listened to Premier Kissof and then said, 'We've done all that, Dimitri. Please believe me. That is the target . . . Yes, they'll understand if they see the recall code in lights . . . All right, I'll wait for your news.'

The President put down the phone and lit another cigarette. At this moment there was nothing more he could do.

Leper Colony

The wind was blowing in through the many holes in *Leper*

Colony, but King did not feel the cold as he worked hard to keep the bomber close to the ground.

'We've got about nine minutes before we reach the target,' said Kivel.

'That's good,' said King. 'We're going to get there, boys.'

'We've got fuel for twelve minutes,' said Kivel.

King thought about what he should do. He was thinking about this when Zogg spoke.

'King, there's something wrong with the bomb doors.'

'What are you talking about?'

'They must be damaged. I can't open them.'

'That's impossible!'

'I've tried everything. Come and see for yourself.'

King said, 'Dietrich. Do you think you can fly this on two-eight-zero and not hit any trees?'

'Sure,' said Dietrich. He came forward and moved into King's seat. He knew enough to keep the plane in the air. He looked ahead anxiously as King went down to see Zogg.

Zogg moved to the left to let King see the equipment.

'Try it,' he said.

King pressed the switches which controlled the bomb doors. Nothing happened.

'I'm going down there,' he said.

'That's dangerous, King,' said Zogg. 'If those doors open, you might fall out.'

'That's a chance I've got to take,' said King.

He opened a small door in the floor and dropped into the bomb area. Although they were lying flat, the two bombs, *Hi There!* and *Dear John*, were taller than him.

King kicked and jumped on the doors, trying to force them loose. But they refused to open.

As he climbed up the ladder, he put his hands on the bombs and spoke to them.

'Don't worry, old friends. You'll get there.'

King went back to the front of the plane.

'Everything's OK,' said Dietrich, as he moved out of King's seat.

King checked the instruments quickly.

'How long have we got, Kivel?'

'Six minutes.'

'OK,' said King. 'Dietrich, stay here.'

Chapter 14   *Dear John*

The War Room

The President said, 'No contact?'

'No contact, sir,' replied his assistant.

'They should be able to stop one bomber,' said the President.

Turgidson said, 'Well, sir, it's not easy. You've got to remember that that plane is really low. Radar can't follow it.'

Everyone looked at the Big Board. More Russian planes were moving towards America.

Dr Strangelove was writing numbers on a piece of paper. He was certain his idea would work.

Leper Colony

King pulled back on the controls and the bomber started climbing.

He said, 'OK, Dietrich, now you take her up to three thousand metres while I go down again to the bomb doors.'

Dietrich sat down again, and King went back down to the bombs. He remembered a problem with the doors he had experienced once before. This time he knew how to solve the problem. With some difficulty, he climbed on to *Dear John* and found a broken connection. He made the connection and sat down on *Dear John*.

Zogg looked down at him anxiously. He said, 'Are you all right, King?'

'Sure,' said King. He looked carefully at his watch. When he thought they were over their target, he pressed a switch.

Nobody would ever know what went through King's mind in the next few seconds. The bomb doors opened and *Dear John* began to fall. King fell with it, shouting and holding on to his hat.

Three minutes later, *Dear John* exploded.

The Doomsday Machine

Under a mountain in Siberia, computers received information from the explosion.

They examined the information.

They arrived at their decision.

For a few seconds there was silence.

Then there was an explosion that made the bomb from *Leper Colony* look like a child's toy.

Chapter 15   Dr Strangelove's Plan

The War Room

The President put down his phone. He said, 'The bomb has been dropped and the Doomsday Machine has exploded. God knows it's not our fault.'

General Turgidson said, 'It's wrong. You know, I can accept twenty, forty, a hundred million dead, but everybody? It's not right.'

The President said, 'Mr Ambassador, how much time have we got?'

The Ambassador's voice was tired.

'Four, possibly six months in the north. Perhaps a year in the south.'

'Perhaps *not!*'

Everyone turned to the man who had said those words.

It was Dr Strangelove.

The President said, 'What do you mean, Dr Strangelove?'

'Mr President, I think we can save a few people.'

'How?' said the President.

'Under the ground. At the bottom of some of our deepest mines.'

'At the bottom of mines? I don't understand.'

'The effects of the nuclear explosion would not reach a mine that was thousands of metres deep.'

The President looked at him.

'You mean people would stay in there for almost a hundred years? How?'

Dr Strangelove smiled. 'It would not be difficult. Electricity would come from nuclear power. Plants could be grown under glass, and they would make it possible to breathe the air. Animals could be kept for food. We would have to check all the mines in the country to see which ones could be used. I think there would be enough space for several hundred thousand of our people.'

'Only several hundred thousand,' said the President. 'What about all the other people? There would be a lot of fighting.'

'I am sure the army could stop that,' said Strangelove.

President Muffley shook his head.

'But who would take such a decision? Who would choose the people to live in the mines?'

Strangelove said, 'There would have to be a special group to study the problem and to suggest how they would be chosen.'

'But how can anyone decide a thing like that?' said the President.

Strangelove said, 'Of course, the people would need to be young, healthy, intelligent and able to have children. They would have different necessary skills, and, of course, they would need to be led by our top government and military men.'

The men were listening to Dr Strangelove very carefully.

'And,' Strangelove continued, 'to have children, there would need to be a lot of women. If there were ten women to each man, the population would grow from two hundred thousand to more than a hundred million when they came out one hundred years later.'

General Turgidson said quietly to his assistant, 'You know, I'm beginning to think this German has got a very good idea.'

The President said, 'But listen, Strangelove, won't these people be shocked and upset that everyone else is dead? They won't want to live.'

'That won't be a problem, sir,' said Strangelove. 'When they go down into the mine, everyone else will still be alive. They will have no shocking memories. It will be an adventure for them.'

General Turgidson looked at Strangelove.

'You said there would be ten women to each man,' he said. 'Wouldn't that mean the end of traditional sexual relationships?'

'I'm afraid so,' said Dr Strangelove, 'but it will be necessary. And because each man will have to have sex with ten women, the chosen women will have to be very sexually attractive.'

The Russian Ambassador said enthusiastically, 'Strangelove, I must say that this is an excellent idea.'

'Thank you, sir.'

General Turgidson said, 'Mr President?'

'Yes, General Turgidson.'

'Mr President, I think we've got to think about this as military commanders too. If the Russians keep some big bombs and we don't, when they come out in a hundred years, they could destroy us.'

General Faceman said, 'I agree, Mr President. In fact, they might try to move into our mine.'

General Turgidson said loudly, 'We must stop them, Mr President!'

ACTIVITIES

Chapters 1–2

Before you read

1 Answer these questions. The words in *italics* are all in the story. Check their meaning in your dictionary.

  a These people are all US *military* officers. Number them from 1 (most important) to 4 (least important).

  colonel   general   lieutenant   major

  b A *base* and a *target* are both places. Which one do *nuclear missiles* and military planes fly from? Which one do they fly to?

  c Is a country's *security threatened* by a friend or an enemy?

  d How are these useful in a plane? An *intercom*, a *navigator* and *radar*.

  e If a military commander wants to *recall* soldiers to base without the enemy's knowledge, which of these is useful? A *cigar* or a *code*?

  f Why, in the past, did some people have to live in a *leper colony*?

2 The film of *Dr Strangelove* appeared in 1964. Its full title is *Dr Strangelove or: How I learned to stop worrying and love the bomb*. What exactly were people worried about at that time?

After you read

3 How do the men on *Leper Colony* feel:

  a at the beginning of the story? Why?

  b when they receive their first message? Why?

  c when they receive their second message? Why?

4 Goldberg says, 'I believe they hit us!' Who are *they* and who are *us*? Is he right?

Chapters 3–5

Before you read

5 General Turgidson is going to a meeting to discuss what General Ripper has done. What do you think he will say?

6 Find these words in your dictionary. Use a form of the words to complete the sentences below.

ambassador   automatic   cancel   emergency
explode   injured   retaliate

a General Turgidson had to leave his secretary because of an ......

b When the bombers reach the Fail-Safe point, they usually return ......

c If General Ripper's order is not ....., the bombers will attack Russia.

d If they attack, Russia will ......

e If a bomb ....., people can be killed or ......

f When a government wants to talk to another government, it often sends a message through its ......

After you read

7 Who:

   a is the only person who can communicate with the bombers?

   b wants to recall the bombers?

   c wants to attack the Russians?

8 Are these sentences true or false? Correct the false sentences.

   a The Russians have attacked.

   b General Ripper wants the President to send more planes to attack Russia.

   c General Turgidson thinks they will be able to recall the planes.

   d Group Captain Mandrake is unhappy with Ripper's plan.

   e Communists are attacking Burpelson.

Chapters 6–8

Before you read

9 President Muffley has invited the Russian Ambassador to the War Room. What do you think they will say to each other?

10 These words are in the story:

doomsday   fluoride   fuel   vodka

Which one:

   a is needed by cars and aeroplanes?

   b is good for your teeth?

   c is a drink?